Fables

from

The South Seas

Kez Wickham St George

Dedication

This book was written for the child that sleeps within your heart, the feeling of happiness that still peeps out at Christmas and birthdays. To the grown-up who still wants to sing Christmas carols and enjoys the excitement of a birthday cake and candles. Writing this book brought forth so many beautiful memories of my own childhood; it was written because, as adults today, more than ever, we all still need that fable or fairy story that has a happy ending. Perhaps when you're tucked up in your own bed, and the night sky is dark, when all in the house are asleep, you will read a story from this book, and it will bring back your memories when 'Once upon a time.' It is also to my forever friend Valeric Shelia, whose faith in the fairy kingdom has never been rattled by others' beliefs. It is to the days when we both navigated adulthood, when our young families filled our homes with laughter, tears, and their own special magic. It is to the healing power of friendship. To the Magic of Friendships and Storytelling.

Index

The Sobstone Bird

Fable 1

In The Very Beginning

My name, Raven, was once great and revered. We were the harbingers of hope and charity; we Ravens were the ones who guided the spirits of the deceased to safety on the other side of life. We were cherished beyond belief. Once, it was customary for a Raven to be invited to live with a family, no matter the title, from the king to the penniless. We Ravens never refused, for only we knew of the promised riches one would have on the other side of death's curtain if a Raven adopted you. The invitation was always issued with great pomp and ceremony, with prayers, music, feasting, and a celebration of joining between two tribes, the Raven and the people. But today, a sudden change of heart from within the people had begun; they now called us the Sobstone birds, for we had become feared on this planet. I admit my cry is now more mournful, like a sobbing child. It seems the people had forgotten the sacred law of community. Now, they lived with debauchery, greed, and war. We, the Ravens, had warned them of the consequences. They had turned on us, maiming our beaks and bodies, they had hunted us into near extinction; the smaller birds of light sweet song had long departed. And I, the only remaining one of the Sobstone birds.

Today, if my sobbing were heard, it would open a flood of fear in one's heart; today, superstitions abounded as my sobbing washed into people's ears. The story now told was, if a sobstone bird was heard, death was close by. And if you were unlucky to see one, its bright blue eye staring at you from within its headdress of the ruffled blue - black feathers, it was advised you liberally sprinkled salt across doorsteps and windowsills and under beds. Prayer flags, beads, and other so-called protection ornaments would be scattered around the grounds and homes or hung high in bare branches or eaves.

It was also declared that malevolence lurked in every shadow of leaf and bush if I was seen in or near your home or garden. Sightings of me, bought nothing but ill health, and bad luck followed in my footsteps. Fear breeds hate, hate breeds violence. Gratefully, I had become the protected pet of one Elder, who still practised and believed in the old lore that to love another, then self-love came first, to love with a happy heart brought magic into your life. Sadly, to the people, the magic of our existence had been forgotten.

However, this story begins when time was not dictated by man or instrument. Only when you looked up into the heavens to the rising sun or setting moon did it tell you of time. Millions of other bright planets still swirled in a galaxy of misty colours. Some planets had burnt to a dull brown or a dusty grey, the inhabitants had long gone either to other homes or had died along with the planet.

It seemed as if a planet imploded into itself, as it crumbled to ash in the heavens; there would be a moment's grieving silence, a whispered sigh of sadness throughout the universe. But if the brightest of stars were born, then celebrations occurred as the heavens rejoiced in the beauty of a star's birth.

On my once beauteous home, it was fast becoming a dead grey orb that was now into its last days of its decay. The "Gods had forsaken us", the people cried as they prepared to flee. They fought and argued over who would be the chosen ones to leave this doomed planet. Discord, blame, and shame travelled the streets. Once upon a time, the people had lived in harmony; all had rejoiced as one tribe, and the people had loved the inhabitants and their homeland. Now the people were fleeing for better, brighter worlds; this planet was no longer useful. My sobs of grief were for the people and the land, it echoed across the tops of mountains and deep ranges, where was their love of this planet we once called home?

They had once lived in happiness, settled within craggy forested mountains, surrounded by waterfalls of misty beauty, an abundance of food, and the land filled with an array of wildlife. Where nobles had built tall castles of stone and marble, but these also had begun to crumble into decay. And although the wise had warned them many times of their wrongdoing, they had continued to rob this planet of its natural resources and riches. Today, nothing but grey dust eddied in waves across the bare pockmarked earth.

However, in their rush to leave, they had forgotten a seedling from the tallest of trees in their once magnificent forests. They had called this tree the upside-down tree, where we all, man-beast or insect, could once seek shelter and food. Sadly, the greed of the inhabitants had destroyed this mighty tree and its surrounds for its treasures. It had been my elder, one of great age, who had found this one remaining seedling struggling to survive amongst the debris and chaos. As tears slipped down her deeply seamed face, she pleaded for this one small plant to be taken to another place, where it hopefully would be protected and loved by the inhabitants.

Her pleas reached those of importance; however, it seemed too hard as they promptly ignored her pleading, saying, "It was of no importance, we are busy with other duties." These very words shook her to the core; she had known for a long time that they did not care, for her or for me her sobstone bird, but a seed? a pure lifeform? How dare they.

Muttering to herself, "What ignorant fools they were, did they not know that this one seed was the beginning of a life?" but she knew to object to this decision would be futile. They were leaving in droves; no invitation was offered to her to depart with them, along with others she was to be sacrificed. In anger, she cursed them, "Your words will be your downfall." Her words were sucked in by a howling wind then released over the queue waiting to leave. Many plans passed through her mind. The carrier of this plant would have to be strong, withstand many elements of wind, ice, and fire; it would know that this was a sacred duty, and this duty may mean its own death. She knew she was incapable of such a journey, the only feasible thought of a saviour kept returning. I, her beloved Raven, her muse, and friend, would be the seedling's bearer. Somehow, she would make it work. It must, for this one seed would prove to give life to many.

My elder begged for a safe passage for me, her Raven, those who governed denying her saying "To be rid of the ugly sobbing creature and the elder would be a relief." Some people sniggered, "Good riddance, some spat at her, others warded off the evil eye with fingers crossed behind their backs or stroked an amulet on their necks or wrists. I watched, my heart heavy, as the hurt to her heart flitted into her eyes, where was the respect she was due, as healer and oracle, she had made many people well with hope and health. Then I saw an understanding written across her face, that she alone was meant to carry out this one last duty, it was crucial that from this planet of death and destruction, both Raven and seedling must find a new home. I also sobbed out my sadness for the wretched sentence passed out to this elder, who only ever wanted peace and harmony to return. She fetched the seedling, stumbling in the fury of the howling wind to find a safe haven; her own home of wattle and bricks had already sunk into a whirlpool of mud, a wind whipping the muddied grit, inflaming her eyes, coated her skin and teeth, it tore at her clothing, her hands barely keeping myself and this small treasure of life safe.

A small cave was found, the wind not quite reaching its shallow depth, placing me on a stone ledge. The elder began to sing the language of the ancient ones, who had first sung the magic of life into this planet. Her song curled around me, giving me faith and hope to reach a planet of safety, to bury the seedling so deep that it would never fear for its life again. Then, she anointed me as this plant's saviour.

As the elder sang, I felt my own eyes begin to glaze with the hypnotic tune, my eyelids began to close, my body swayed to the chant she uttered, and I felt the heat of her face close to mine as she crooned the melody of life that was buried inside this seed. I understood my own purpose given to me at my birth.

Soon, the elder became exhausted, for she understood the purpose; the question was how to complete the task? The earth shuddered and trembled under her body, the cave moaned in urgent distress. When the shifting ground under her body caused her to drop her flask of water, a mud puddle formed, her "Annoyance at being so clumsy" was spoken. It came to her, quickly scraping the mud into her hand then encasing the seedling inside, an oval shape was formed. She began to search my body, spreading my wings open, inspecting my clawed feet, shaking her head, "There is nowhere to attach it." In frustration I began to sob, when she saw a way, placing the tiny clay egg into my open beak.

It was time to farewell each other. She stood, grunting with tiredness as her old body shambled to rise, her bent, trembling fingers stroked my feathers as pebbles and stones showered into her grey hair, "It's time", she sighed. She lifted me high; tears streaked her face as she said, "Find peace and safety my little one."

The cave gave off a groaning yawn, melting into rock and rubble with one dusty, roaring belch as I flew upwards, finding my way into the bruised, coloured skyline. As I looked back, the cave had swallowed the lone figure, and I, the Sobstone bird with its cargo of hope, took to the air.

In flights with my Raven family in the past, we had seen one small planet so bright and beautiful; my instincts drew me closer. I flew through massed clouds, widely passing a planet of fire, spewing its molten fury into space. Soon, passing a large silvered orb, my shadow cast across its bare surface. I flew with great speed through a myriad of stars, then being buffeted by eddying winds and jagged rocks. I felt my endeavours to be successful failing my mission had become futile. I was at the point of exhaustion when a great explosion came from behind me, catching me, tumbling my body in circles, a cruel pain coursed through me, I wanted to sob, but if I did, then all would be lost.

Then, the planet of beauty I knew existed appeared, as it revolved it showed off her amazing colours of green, white, and blue. Soon, I could see the tallest of red-coloured mountains, swarms of birds I had thought long gone; greeted me. The one I heard above them all was one of my own "Raven, welcome." My heart swelled in gratitude; my name was not forgotten. With a sob, I released the clay orb, burying it in the softest of white sand, surrounded by ferns and grasses, beside a lake of blue, the site fed from the mist of a waterfall. I rested, enjoying the cool wind; I then joined the Ravens in their song, it was one of joy, happy in the knowledge that we together would watch this seedling grow into a mighty tree. Here, the seed would flourish and grow, giving life to the many creatures that lived on this new planet, they called Gondwana.

Motto

For The Sobstone Bird

While creating this story, it came to me that the warnings and messages that we are receiving every day have not changed, and that we as a human race are in fact poisoning our own home planet, we call Earth. Not only in the skies and oceans, but our very soil. We as humans are at war with each other. Always ready to accuse and blame, and no matter how many leaks we seem to plug with gratitude, kindness, and love, those who rule seem bent on becoming known as the blue planet that destroyed itself in every way. Maybe one day this will be reversible, who knows? However, no one can say "We were not warned. And maybe this short story will reach the ears of another who will ask the simple question

"How do we mend what we have intentionally broken?"

The Wicklow's

Fable 2

Once Upon A Time

There lived two old folk, known as the Wicklow's, a family of ancient beings that had lived inside the trunk of the mighty Totara tree in a place called Taitokerau. Over the decades, a fable about the Wicklow's had grown, a story that some feared and some loved, some dared to find out if the truth had been spoken, and others scoffed, calling them untruths. People had searched for many days for proof of the Wicklow's existence, but only when the full moon rose and shone down, trickling its light through leaf-filled branches.

And only if you were very still and very quiet, if you looked very closely, letting the mist of humanity lift from your eyes, you would see the Wicklow's tiny figures doing what they did best, mending broken toys. You would hear the faint Tik-Tok of a hammer, or the buzz of a machine; when the weather turned cold, the smell of a pinecone fire may just drift under your nose.

The Wicklow's were known far and wide; they had been the parents of many children who had left the tree house long ago, and now they brought their own children to visit. To all family, friends, and community they were known as Randad & Mamie. Ranrad Wicklow could fix any toy imagined, from tiny little wooden trucks to small Rocking horses, spinning tops, blackboards, and pirate swords. Mamie was the Wicklow who painted the toys with bright colours, sewing new dresses for the dolls or giving them new hair and eyelashes, often into the small hours of the night you would see a light shining from a chink within the tree trunk, especially around a celebration time,

Sometimes if your footsteps were quiet, you could hear Mamie singing as she sewed the dolls dresses or filled the dollies bark tubes of legs and arms with a soft mossy stuffing, often a smile would tug at her creased cheeks when she remembered the joy on a child's face when the once broken doll was reclaimed by the owner and loved once again. Mamie was also known for her calming unguents, if a forest child had a fall, grazing their knees or elbows, Mamie's unguents would soon be used to start the healing process. However, if it were an emergency, Randad Wicklow would harness his two pet possums to a wooden sleigh, racing over hill and dale to find the help they needed. One day, Mamie climbed to the top branch of the Totara tree, where she had seen some forest mushrooms growing on a branch, which would make a tasty meal.

However, when she looked out into the horizon, she saw many strange new buildings being built, she had seen it happen to other friends in their habitats, forcing them to flee to find another place to exist unharmed, it made her feel very uncomfortable, as her nature called for the love and peace within the quiet of this forest. This was where she had been born and where she would pass away, at one with her forest.

Everyday they became busier than ever, Ranrad's tiny drills and hammers never seeming to stop, Mamie's needles, pins and paint brush seemed to fly through the air from the early morning hours, till later than dusk as they both worked away at their tasks.

The usual payment for their work had been a jar of honey or a basket of mushrooms or acorns, lately, the two of them had more than they could possibly eat, their home bulged with baskets filled with food and acorn pots that overflowed with golden honey. Mamie had begun to give the food away to the other Wicklow families, making sure that when the cold winds and rain of winter arrived, all pantries would be full.

However, not all felt safe, and uneasiness filled the air around her. All through the Spring, summer, and Autumn, she had felt the spirits of this forest were unhappy. Finally, she shared her thoughts with Ranard, as today she noticed not one bird sang amongst the branches, not one bright orange winged butterfly had flown past, no one had called out a greeting, and not one furred or winged forest child slept within the empty nests of fallen leaves. To herself she had explained the unusual silence, as a hot summer plus some friends and family had left for a cooler climate. But this silence went deeper; in their hearts, they knew their people were leaving because of the humans moving closer.

They also knew once the humans arrived peace and harmony and the many winged friends that protected this forest would also leave; a sliver of fear crept into the ancient Wicklow's hearts.

A holiday at a seaside village called Ngunguru was planned, written on a wooden sign in big red letters 'closed until our return' was hung from a large nail on their front door. Mamie had closed all the window shutters that let in the soft forest light. Their home fire was extinguished and the tallest of the Totara tree fell silent. With a deep sigh, the two ancient Wicklow's packed a case, harnessed their possums to the wooden sleigh; just as they were about to leave, a huge truck stopped beside their tree home, one human got out and sprayed a bright pink X on the trunk. The Wicklow's knew it was time to leave, and as they quickly hurried away; smaller trees began to fall around them.

They both had heard whispers that this was being done to warm and house the humans, who did not seem to care that they were invading a (tapu), a sacred place. Ranrad had never felt such rage, insults about the human's carnage fell from his lips, he snapped the whip above the Possums heads, yelling 'Ride.' His blue eyes bright with angry tears, Mamie held tight to her bonnet of ferns and sparrow feathers.

She had no words to describe the great melancholy that had buried itself in her heart, nor could she speak of her heartbreak, wondering where their spirits would go. If their ancestors were no longer there to greet and guide them? Would they be forever lost in the great white clouds of Aotearoa?

Both Wicklow's knew that a return to the old home and their ways would disappear once their ancient tree was cut down, it was with a deep sadness they continued their journey. For two days they travelled over hill and dale, through thick bush and dark forests. Then one day, as the sun shone and the smell of sea air tickled their noses, they found a grass meadow, large wooden posts dotted the edge. Ranrad spied a thick wooden post with a large round knotty hole at its base, it was perfect for them to holiday in. However, Mamie's heart remained with her beloved Totara tree.

She cried out in pain feeling it in her bones when the tree fell, she heard the soft moan as it gave up its spirit, she felt its sacred heart splinter apart. Mamie's tears ran down her wrinkled cheeks, her hiccupping sobs echoed around the room, nothing consoled her heartache, Ranrad became concerned for his Wicklow's heart, for her life light shivered with grief of what once was.

Three mornings passed when Mamie could not arise, on the fourth morning all was not well, Ranrad expected the worst, Mamie lay there her chest barely rising with each breath, when she heard a sound that grounded her fears, lit her eyes and warmed her heart, her prayers had been answered. Their family of daughters, son's, nieces, nephews, cousin's, aunties, uncles, and grandchildren had followed them, all chorusing one of her teachings as she joined them 'Families that play together, stay together.'

Scooping up a new grandbaby to cuddle, her heart settled, she knew that when her day came to leave this world, her ancestors would find her, to welcome, guide and cherish. And to this day, amongst the old knotty wooden fenceposts that dot the seaside village of Ngunguru, if you stop and listen, you will hear the Wicklow's. It may sound like a faint birdcall or a reed pipe being played in the distance. Feel no fear for it is the Wicklow's, and as their ancestors once did, they are now the guardians of Taitokerau.

The End

Motto

To The Wicklow's

In all customs throughout the Globe,

family and community are held in highest of regard, for it is within these groups story telling in its purest form takes place. There are many ways of telling stories, Fables carry a message of hope, respect, and kindness towards one another, and consider the belief that when you leave this mortal coil, you will have left a legacy for others to learn from.

Rouget

Fable 3

A Long, Long Time Ago

Her wings slumped in sadness as Roguet leant against the crumbling brick wall of the old bell tower, marvelling at how beautiful it looked in the silvered moonlight. In the daytime, it looked like exactly what it was - a derelict, crumbling, ancient tower. Once, when it had been first built, the bell rang, pealing its deep chime with joy as it called all the surrounding villages together to celebrate the full moon and solstice of the seasons, to feast and dance. Weddings, parties and funerals, no matter the occasion or celebration, the villagers would flock to the Ivy Bell tower.

But today, when you hear people talk about the bell tower, fear is laced in their voices; they say it has become haunted, not with ghosts, but with something more dangerous, the faerie folk. It was said if possessions - even children went missing, it was the fairies. Often told was the tale of tinkling laughter and twinkling lights, disappearing into the tower walls it had had the fairy hunters out more than once. Any mysterious boils, hair loss or coughs or colds in the villages, the people would point to the tower. You would hear the elders mutter 'It's those dammed fairies; life was good till they arrived.' The stories grew wilder; those that visited, became doused in dread, too scared to sleep in case a fairy or elf stole a child or a precious item. Still, this rotting, crooked, old tower that had weathered many years of storms, stood proudly upright on the hill.

It was here Roguet hid from the villagers, she knew she would never be one of them, but if not human then what or who was she? Did one as grotesque as she, have a future? The wind had become sharp and cold, in the darkest corner of the tower a damp bed of leaves and soft grasses welcomed her tired body, her head throbbed with the unanswered questions, to whom and where did she belong? Falling softly to her bedding, her wings folded around her, she dreamt of a world she had once felt safe in.

When the policeman who had jailed her called her, a child of the female sex, a known pickpocket and troublemaker, a street fighter and urchin, he was correct. She had not been given a name at birth, a guttersnipe she was called, as that was where she had been found; in the gutter, like many of her young friends who had roamed the streets with her. Fed by anyone, willing to share or begging scraps from rubbish of the wealthy. She had no status in this society of thieves and cutthroats. She was a nobody, with no name.

When the local judge pointed his grubby finger at her, his bulbous purple veined nose twitching as he stuffed snuff up his black stained nostrils, his sneeze a snot-filled sound like a gunshot over her head, she trembled with fear. The judge pounded a large wooden gavel onto the podium's top, sentencing her to jail. He called out 'You child, are a Rogue' just as his false wooden teeth cracked together, pronouncing it Roguet.

She felt like she had been given a crown, she squared her shoulders; standing tall and proud, as she was led from the docks. To this six-year old's heart she had been given a blessing, at last here was somewhere to lay her head, a meal a day and she had been given her own name, Roguet. She felt gratitude swell in her chest, as she stood in line with other inmates; her prison number was painted on a large wooden disc; to wear around her neck. Now Roguet was someone, the old priest, who painted her numbers on the disc, took his time, his whiskery chin bobbing up and down as he muttered, "You are the 12th child today, and today is the 12th day of the 12th month." He pushed his dirty face close to hers, his rheumy yellowed eyes stared into hers, his breath rank with the smell of his rotten teeth, spittle settled on her pale cheeks as he whispered 'them's magic numbers, only the farie folk have magic' his grimy hand settled on her small arm, cruelly pinching her soft flesh; she recognised the malice, as he said "Magic is sin and sinners ave to be punished" her newfound confidence disappearing.

Suddenly, she was pulled away "Come on, ya bag of bones, it's the workhouse for you," the voice wa instantly corrected as Roguet took her first big breath and yelled "My name is Roguet." A silence fell over the room; the hands that had pulled her free; lifted her high, eyes of brightest blue stared into hers. A smile twitched around a full red mouth, "We ave a live one ere ladies, she finks she's a bloody princess. You'll do pet, you can call me Ma." The friendship was sealed immediately. Roguet had never felt safer or happier, soon becoming Ma's shadow. Ma was the one woman that the other cellmates took care not to anger; her wrath was fast and furious, and many heads had been cracked against the damp walls of the cell. Roguet slept tucked across Ma's lap, their share of any food carefully guarded by Ma. It was when Ma was marched off to the guard's room that Roguet felt fear; veiled threats against them both would slide over and around her, she would shrink into the darkest of corners, her eyes squeezed shut, praying no one would take this life away from her.

Ma would disappear once or twice a week, Rouget once and only once bravely asking 'could she go with her,' it was the first time her Ma had slapped her and shouted "Never; wish for that." For some reason Ma was a favoured one amongst guards, on her return she would carry a jug of grey greasy cold water. With this, she would first wash Roguet and then herself. If there was food to share on her return, Ma would make sure it was divided equally amongst the cellmates. Roguet always receiving the bigger share. Ma once commented, "Why ain't you grown, Pet? You been stunted by your life?"

Once, when Ma had returned to the cell, her face smeared in blood, a tooth was missing, but she held up a prize, a jug of clear water, plus a small grubby sack was produced. Ma had already torn holes in it for Roguet's head to fit through and for the 'skinniest arms in the world' as Ma had said. First a wash, was ordered, the sacking used for a rough drying off, then pulled over Roguet's head, it fell to the floor, Ma tore a strip off her torn stained petticoat, winding it around Rougets waist, "A dress for a princess" she said. The insults and jeers from others in the cell stopped when Ma stood and crossed her arms.

Rouget knew she was safe beside her beloved saviour. When the day came and Ma was set free, Roguet shivered with anxiety. No one liked her; what would she do without her protector and friend? When the guard yelled, prisoner number three was free to go. Ma's large, rough hand reached for her, steadying her as she whispered, "Quiet now, Pet. I've been here too long; no one remembers who did what."

Most villages shooed them away as they approached asking for food or work, "Abuse and rocks were hurled at them. Ma headed into the hills; Roguet became exhausted, no food or drink had been found or was offered.

Ma hoisted her onto her broad back; it was dusk when a shallow cave was found. Wearily, Ma sank down onto the dirt floor, stroking the small child's hair "Don't fret Pet, it's only for the night." The first night had been cold and wet with rain and wind reaching into the cave; Ma had done her best to protect the child, curling her body around Roguet's tiny one. Once the sun was up Ma had woken her, together they watched the mist lift, fields of flowers appeared. Both delighting in the beauty, everywhere was bright with perfumed colour. Trees so tall with crowns of green leaf they seemed cloud bound, the musical sound of running water was close by. 'We's be alright here Pet, there's a lot to live on ere,' Ma worked hard that day, first tickling a river trout for a meal, Roguet stroked the soft body, adoring the colours rippling across its scales, squealing with terror as it flicked its body, turning away in distress when Ma gutted and cleaned it for their meal. Together they collected bush and grasses to gather for their bed; she was shown how to collect kindling and dry wood.

Building the fire had fascinated Roguet, as Ma knelt on the dirt floor rubbing two sticks together, puffing air into the tiny swirl of smoke, grunting in her efforts, a loud noise erupted from Ma's backside. Roguet's laughter had bounced off the cave walls. They both stopped and stared at each other as it was the first time Roguet had ever laughed out loud. Ma's eyes became soft, reaching out to her charge, she cuddled Roguet's small frame, "Never craved to be a Ma, now look at me, soft as porridge over a rag-bag of bones." The fire warmed everything, making the walls glow with orange, warming their bodies; the dried pinecones collected that day, opened with the heat, Ma shook the seeds from them, making sure they were cool enough to snack on; Roguet had never tasted anything so delicious.

For the first time in her life, Roguet ate baked fish, her mouth was not used to the texture or smell, she struggled with it, but to please Ma she persevered. When nausea washed over her, Ma's grumbled about "Waste not want not" as Roguet spat it out, retching repeatedly as her tummy rejected the soft white meat. The drink of fresh cool water soon settled the nausea. Roguet's eyes fluttered to sleep listening to Ma tell stories of her own childhood, promising that tomorrow they would have a bath, the cave had become their home.

That promise was kept the next day. Ma walked into the pool first, Roguet stood on the grassy shore, crippled with fear. When Ma said, "Come'er Pet, time to rid you of that stink of Jail," The pale child dipped one toe into the pool. It was freezing! Ma grabbed her hand pulling her in, Roguet opened her mouth to scream, it filled with water so cold it took her breath away. Ma held her close, rocking her body close to hers in the cold water "It's okay Pet, we's free ere, we av food, each other, were ome." Weeks turned into months, the summer into autumn. Ma had taught her how to weave the field flowers into a chain then place them on her head, "A crown for me princess" Ma would joke. Often when the chores had been done, they would lie on their backs gazing up at the sky, Ma pointing out clouds shaped like an animal or bird.

Some days Roguet would wander through the fields, then telling Ma about the birds and animals scurrying about in the trees and fields. The weather was getting colder, Ma saying the animals were gathering food for the winter and that they should do the same. Together they found pinecones and kindling, grasses were gathered for fresh bedding; Ma taught Rouget how to weave a screen door, life was good. When winter was beginning to nip their toes, the cave became a warm haven; no one bothered them.

Ma had begun going for walk's once or twice a week, claiming it was to beg for bread or cheese, Roguet's job was to stay inside the cave, under strict orders to not wander away or go to the pool on her own, to watch the fire and make sure their cave was safe.

When Ma was returning, she would wave her pinny in the air, a signal she was not far away. Her smile trying to make light of a bruise on her face or body, but always in Ma's pocket the promised chunk of heavy brown bread or potted meat, or a hunk of yellow cheese. Roguet learnt not to ask how or why? If she did Ma would scowl - her anger roaming around them for a day. It was soon understood between them Roguet did not like the taste of any flesh, so when Ma bought home a small clay pot of honey, with a chunk of coarse bread, Roguet fell in love with the taste and texture.

Ma looked on with delight as this wan child gobbled it up, her grubby little fingers trickling long sticky strands of honey onto the stale bread, licking her lips with big smacking sounds. It was a late afternoon when Ma suggested a dip in the pool, the seasons were changing and cooler, but today the sun dappled water was enticing. Ma went in first, dipping under the water, rubbing coarse sand from the bottom of the pool over her own body.

The fear of water had left Roguet; she stripped off her faded sack and waded in beside Ma, copying Ma's actions, first a handful of sand then a good scrubbing, till their bodies glowed pink. When Ma had asked Roguet to rub sand over her back, she did so; Ma's strong body now shiny wet, her skin showing a pink gold tinge in the sunset. Then it was Roguet's turn; this was one of her favourite things in the pool, to have her back rubbed with sand, she waited in pleasant anticipation, her eyes half closed, her body relaxed. Ma's hand stopped still on Roguet's back, 'Pet, you have two small lumps on your back, are they sore? Ma quickly pulled her out of the pool; Roguet now stood on the leafy bank of the pool shivering, Ma hands examining her small body. 'Oh, dear God, not the plague,' Ma whispered, her hand quickly searching under Roguet's armpits, under her hairline and jaw, then her groin, searching for the telltale lumps.

Questions shot out of Ma's mouth, "Are you aching, pet? Do you feel squeamy in the belly? What colour are your waters? Are you shaky? Roguet shook her head to each question. "Ma stop; you're hurting me.' Ma cupped her face up in one hand, her words soft and clipped 'if you feel sick you will tell me, yes?

Roguet nodded, asking for more honey. Ma was so relieved there was no sign of any disease, "Of course, pet, only the fairies love the honey like you do." She no sooner uttered those words then it all made sense, the tiny body that never seemed to grow into childhood, the child's intuition in the woods of what to eat, the disgust shown when Ma devoured meat or fish. Ma's pet glowed with health; she lived on a diet of nuts, berries, and seeds, in fact, Ma had noticed Roguet copied what the creatures around them ate, drinking what they drank from the pool. That night as they curled together on their bed of bracken, the fire warming their feet, Ma remembered what she had said out loud about the fairies, quietly berating herself, for it was common knowledge, to be careful what you say in the woods, you never know who's listening.

However, she would keep a close eye on her small charge until she was certain there was no danger. Everyone knew that harbouring a child that was fay was dangerous. The past summer together, they both worked hard, knowing the winters here were merciless, driving snow and rain into their home.

Today, the weaved door was pulled over the mouth of the cave, both had curled up on the bed of bracken, the small fire keeping them warm. Roguet was always happy when these days occurred; it had become Ma's storytelling time. So, after a story of make believe, they had both fallen into a deep sleep, when Ma was woken by the sound of rapid chatter coming to a stop outside the cave.

Rising quietly so the child would not wake, Ma peered through the cracks of the cane screen, the rain and wind had stopped, an eerie silence had settled. Outside winking lights floated amongst the trees, each light being held by a person no bigger than a finger on her hand, they whispered and giggled and sang amongst each other, then silence as a sleek miniature pale grey horse with a long-twisted horn of cream ivory on its forehead, walked daintily up to the cave door. On its back sat a young man, his face handsome, waves of black hair fell past his shoulders, draping softly down his body. His skin shone green the colour of emeralds. Ma's heart skipped a beat, she knew from the stories of her own childhood who he was, the king of all fairies, Oberon.

Then another miniature horse appeared - this time from the canopy of trees, its body, and wings as black as night. The beautiful women that sat on its back needed no description, it was Titania - bride of Oberon, this was the young man's Queen. Her long silver hair was streaked with diamonds it floated around her body like a silver cloak. As she dismounted, she stroked her horse's wings, speaking softly in the language of ancient times, the words hypnotic. The twinkling lights dipped as the knees of many that floated in the trees, bent before their king. Ma's heart was hammering, fear making her shiver; she had nothing to offer them, she wanted to be sick. It was common knowledge amongst village folk how vengeful the faerie people could be if not pleased. As the royal couple swept into the cave, Ma looked around, now she saw it through their eyes, she and Roguet lived like animals of the forest. She had not tidied or swept this day because of the rain and wind, it smelt of old burnt wood, sour bodies and damp rocks, shame joined the fear which curled inside her. Titania and Oberon stood as tall as Ma's knee, their power filled the cave.

"You have one of us with you? Asked Oberon, his voice sounded almost childish. Ma mutely nodded. By this time, Roguet had woken, her eyes becoming huge with excitement. Titania held out her hand, which Rouget accepted. Silence took place as Titania studied the child, "You are to be complimented on your mercy for this little one, but she is not one of us." Ma looked confused, "Then who is she? Titania shrugged, "It is not for us to say, why do we not feast together and ponder over this dilemma?" With a snap of the king's emerald-covered fingers, the cave became filled with the winking lights, the line of fairies now busy producing a meal of splendour. Instantly, rich green carpets of moss covered the cave floor while plump white fungi became large soft cushions. Dishes of fruit, pots of honey, silver goblets of clear water sat beside small bronze plates; each one heaped high with sweet breads.

Oberon assisted his bride Titania to sit; he then offered his hand to Ma inviting her to "Sit with them and partake of our food." Roguet loved the gentle music the fairies played, her body swayed to the sound of soft flutes, bells, and drums. She had waited politely as Ma had taught her; however, she had not been invited to join them in this meal, so when her hand had strayed to a plate of pretty cakes, her fingers closed around dirt and small twigs. She tried once more thinking it was a trick of her mind, the plate of cakes was right before her, once more, her hand gathered only dirt and dried twigs.

As she went to warn Ma of the magic, the dancing began, a party of such joy swung around her, the warning and hunger was forgotten, she simply had to join in, never having any cause to dance before; Roguet copied the skipping steps by the fairies, linking arms, weaving in and out of an unseen pattern.

With a flick of the Queens wrist, flowers adorned Roguet's hair, the sack cloth became a floating sheath of blue gossamer, the protruding lumps on her back seemed to wriggle free of their pale skin covering, her small down covered wings fluttered free, she felt as light as thistle down, her laughter joined the others. Happiness filled the cave, too soon the music stopped, the cave once full of sound and laughter was silenced, the fairies settled down in a semi-circle. An older faerie stood on top of a log by the open fire; he cleared his throat, looking straight into Roguet's eyes. All other noise had been hushed as this lone tiny man began to recite.

His ancient voice crept into Roguet's chest, she knew it was meant for her and her alone.

The wishing stone hides beneath yon tree
no longer seen by all who see.
Once its surface a glinting silver
Dulled with greed by youth of age,
only shines brightly for a known sage.
All elders know with sight unseen.
Not all ask for grass's green.
They demand strength, wealth, and power.
Pleas to have magic stirred in their blood,
Unleashed a spell, turning their world sour
The stone of wishes lies beyond yon door.
Only a true of heart can step through its shield.
Be careful what you wish for, it may not be for you.
Only the pure of heart will prove this to be true.

Ma sat quietly talking to the royal couple, occasionally looking up and smiling at the child she thought of as her own, her eyes widening in surprise when she saw the downy wings protruding from her back, but saying nothing - knowing that whatever happened now, was meant to be. Ma's eyes became heavy and with a huge sigh: she rolled onto her side and began to snore. There were a few titters around the room silenced by the look on Oberon's face. The royal couple stood, the party had ended, the cave reverted back to a dirt floor and damp walls, the fire spluttered to a stop.

Oberon spoke to Rouget, "You are not of the fairy world, and you are not part of the human world" Make your choice now, leave with us or stay and be hunted, until your own kind seek you out." Roguet knew they were being truthful; she knew the hunters were close, she knew those bruises Ma had laughed off as being clumsy was untrue. Ma's smile was no longer bright, she had heard Ma sob with pain as she lay in the water, the cold water soothing her bruised body. She knew her Ma had been protecting her, however once the onset of age or illness began; their roles would change, Ma would become her responsibility, and their lives would become difficult. Roguet asked for one thing, 'that Ma was given her wish for a grand life, never wanting again.' Oberon nodded, then he warned her, 'In return, our magic always asks for an innocent's tear.' Roguet nodded in agreement.

Titania walked over to the woman who slept deeply. She raised her tiny, jewelled hands over Ma's body and sang.

'All you wish for from the deep goodness of your heart is yours today as we do part. No fretting or worry shall ever be yours. The life you wish for is through an open door. Your dreams will carry you to welcoming arms. Sleep on, dear heart, and want no more.'

As Roguet left the cave, a blanket of moss had begun to cover Ma's body, pillowy mushrooms of purest white cradled her head, over the entrance to what was once Rougets home, boulders creaked and rumbled into place, a large tree began to grow in the entrance blocking off the world of magic as Ma was left safe to forever dream, the world of humankind never to hurt or harm her again. The price asked for was paid, Roguet's heartbroken tears fell freely as she farewelled her Ma.

Roguet was escorted by the long twinkling line of fairy lights to the Bell tower, setting beside her a small bowl of nectar and a bladder of water, the sheath of blue gossamer still clung to her body, the perfume of flowers still hung in the air. She was told to wait, but every creak or crack, whisper or squeak terrified her. As she had waited, alone in the tower, her wings became covered with soft blue-black feathers, she longed to stretch them, her thoughts becoming resentful 'if I have wings, then why can I not fly away from here? Her intuition reminding her, where would I go?

Roguet felt the shadow stand over her before she was awake, fear rushed through her body, she shrieked in fear, her first thoughts were 'they have caught me and will kill me.' Strong arms encased her body holding her firmly, a male voice demanding she stop struggling. Once her eyes had cleared of sleep, she saw who knelt beside her. Another just like her in every way, his voice spoke with kindness "I'm not here to harm you, Oberone sent us a messenger, you are one of us." Rougets questions of what and who barely asked, when he replied "I, like you are an earth-bound sprite, my name is Dantento, you were once known to us as Whitestem, I'm here to bring you home." His dark wings beat with a steady rhythm as they together they rose; she had looked up into his face seeking the dislike from others she had become used to. Relief flooding her heart when his eyes showed nothing but kindness and empathy. Roguet felt no fear, only relief that one just like her had rescued her. As they rose into the dusk of night she asked one request, to say one last goodbye to her saviour and friend Ma.

Wishing for just one more time she could be with her beloved Ma. Dantento pointed to a large silver rock at the base of the tree. "There is a wishing stone Whitestem" she then remembered what the older fairy had sung, it all made sense and as she caressed the stone, an image slowly appeared in her mind, it was Ma, she was smiling, waving her pinny in the air, walking towards her in a field filled with flowers, she knew her beloved Ma's spirit would never be wanting or in danger ever again. Their wings opened in unison as they rose into the golden dawn of a new day, a single ray of sunlight glinted off the silver wishing stone.

Motto

Rouget's Story

Rouget's story began as one of defeat. She is a young girl learning to have confidence in others. While her future may look dark, she learns that every tunnel has a light at its end. Her story is about having faith in oneself to discover the true core of who you are, to believe that your presence and your story are important, and to remember that your influence, like your shadow, will be in places you have never been or seen.

The Glass Jar

Fable 4

A Very Long Time Ago

*I*t was a midsummer twilight on a faraway island called Waiheke, when the light of the day shifts to that magical hour, the change of tide and time, when the human will drowse and where the invisible can take shape.

Dragon Lillie, the prettiest butterfly in this forest watched impatiently as the humans that called themselves Gypsies built a camp just under her tree where she and her family lived. As they tethered their horses, the Gypsy children played in the deep forest, some believing the glow bugs were fairies. Each child trying to catch the teeny bright flickering light in glass jars.

The Elders knowing better, warning them, not to catch them, for if they happened to capture one the fairy folk? Well, it was common knowledge they had proved to be difficult, their utterings and spells often coming true, so it was best not to annoy them.

Frustrated, as she wanted to see more, Dragon Lillie, finally flew from the highest of branches to the lowest, watching carefully as her family approached the Gypsies; for the humans had something they all craved. The Gypsies were fascinated by these teeny fragile creatures; wanting to know about them, in return they gave them what they wanted, mead made from wild honey. It was well known that mead made them dance and sing, then become very sleepy. But even more than the powerful drink, Dragon Lillie craved to know more, so she flew from one colourful caravan window to another, peeping inside each one as she flew past.

Suddenly, a hand shot out from a small window; as it tried to grab her, she nipped it with her little teeth, the hand was hastily withdrawn. Dragon Lillie was about to make a dash back her family for safety, the hand once more appeared, this time in an open gesture; "I won't hurt you; I just want to talk with you."

The voice was young, melodic, Dragon Lillie could sense no malice or mischief in the voice, so she decided to settle on the open hand, which belonged to a young girl, who after they had talked about how beautiful her wings were, the young girl gave Dragon Lillie her promised reward, a tiny spoon of golden mead to drink.

With a large yawn, a flutter of her wings Dragon Lillie curled up in the palm of the Gypsies' hand; falling into a deep sleep, dreaming of a summer's day, when she would visit the blue bell flowers deep in the forest, rubbing her body against them so her wings glowed with the richness of Indigo. Or, if the Daffodils were out, she would collect the gold pollen from their stamens and powder her wings with the golden dust. The pain woke her; her wings had been cruelly pinched between fingers when she was dropped into a glass jar. The young Gypsy girl taped the jar, "You belong to me now." Dragon Lillie felt betrayed and angry, furiously beating her tiny fists against the glass, which only made them ache. It was then she heard another voice behind her 'it's no use little one, they keep us here: feeding us on honey and water, they swap us between them and show us off to one another, to escape a Glass Jar is rare."

Dragon Lillie whirled around to face who had spoken to her, a large silver blue bush moth lay curled up at Dragon lilies feet. She was about to answer the moth when she knocked off balance as the jar was placed on a shelf, alongside them were many glass jars that held all sorts of creatures, from an assortment of colourful beetles, crickets, ladybugs, and hairy spiders, she saw moths, more butterflies, and bees, all trapped as she was. "They think we are fairies because we fly, they trap us in jars till we no longer amuse them. Occasionally, a kind human sets us free, but that is not common. My name is Moni, please don't be frightened - what's your name? Come, sit beside me, tell me about yourself."

Over time, Moni and Dragon Lillie became friends, and as time passed, they learnt much about each other, but never spoke of the sadness they both felt. they slept curled up around each other, for comfort and care. Then one day Moni could not stand, her legs collapsing under her, they both knew the bush moth was dying. Moni begged Dragon Lillie to try and escape, but Dragon lilies' wings had been damaged. Dragon Lillie sat down beside her friend Moni, placing the moths head on her knees, stroking the small black furry head, both desperately thinking, trying to come up with ideas for an escape.

Suddenly Moni cried out "I know, use my wings, I have not got the strength to escape, but you have Dragon Lillie. "If you don't eat the honey today, you can escape." There was no time to argue, they could hear the jars being taken down off the shelf so the humans could drip honey into them. Dragon Lillie carefully held Monis wings up; they were already beginning to warp with the lack of fresh air and sunshine. Moni quickly undid the front of her silver vest wriggling out of it. Dragon Lillie did the same, noticing that her own wings had also lost their bright freshness.

While Moni wrapped her vest of soft fur around Dragon Lillie, she let her own wings fall, as they fluttered to the bottom of the glass jar; for one terrible second, she felt the welling of grief, a farewell to a beautiful part of her she had treasured for all her short years. Giving her friend one last hug, thanking her for her generosity, Dragon Lillie stretched her new bush moth wings; they were almost too big for her little body, and much too big to open fully inside the Jar.

The top of the jar was pulled open - this was her chance, and as the honey was being replaced, Dragon Lillie quickly leapt, flying up and out, as fast as her new silver blue wings would take her.

The Gypsy dropped the jar and trying to catch her, but Dragon Lillie was too fast. Moni yelling out "Go my friend, fly high." Moni sank to the bottom of the glass jar, her eyes closing, her life was over, but her heart was filled with happiness that her last act was one of helping another to live.

Finally, resting high up in a treetop, the butterfly with the wings of a bush moth watched the caravan leave, her heart heavy with sadness knowing she would never see Moni again, but so grateful she had been given another chance to fly into the treetops. To feel the dappled sunlight on her face, Dragon Lillie rested amongst the leaves, until her new wings were strong and felt just right. Declaring loudly to all that could hear her 'It may be with another's wings that I fly, but they are going to be the best wings any butterfly ever had."

The End

Motto

Of the Glass Jar

I feel in this fable there is a truly clear motto, and that is: always help another when and if you are able. To loan your wings, so to speak, if you are able to help another fly, to reach their dreams and goals, then why not do so? There is something heartwarming when watching another reach their goals, and maybe it was simply because you have invested a little time with them.

The Conductor

Fable 5

Long ago the sun & moon painted the sky
with the colours of purest love for the orb
they named Gaia.

On a small island off the coast of Fiji
a ripple of excitement travels through the
expectant flock of birds that had made
themselves comfortable on the branches of
the ancient Drautabua tree, its bark like an
old unwanted overcoat being shrugged off in
great chunks, its pink belly being displayed
like toothless gums. A hum of settling down,
then quiet; baby birds were being tucked
under the mother bird's wing as dusk
displayed the first star of the night, the
Southern Star. This heavenly beacon was one
of hope and the corner-stone of many fables
and stories. Tonight would be no different;
whether it be story or song, it would be

memorable. The gathering waited, hushed, as a large Blue Herron bird glided majestically onto a branch way up high, making his place known, stepping very stately from one leg to the other, fluffing his wings out then settling down to show off his sleek lines, he preened his chest feathers, moodily muttering his personal complaints of today's annoying issues that he had had no time to deal with.

Knowing they were late, a mad squawking swarm of green and orange Kula's landed, the dusky pink of the sunset highlighting their chests to the colour of coral rose. Their greetings to one another filled the sky with a harsh screeching of noise, pecking, and sniping at each other to gain just the right place. The noise slowly fades as the majestic Heron taps his beak on a branch. With the experience of a professional, this large bird begins to posture, enthralling all, for he is the conductor of the day's farewell.

The flocks of birds become hushed in respect, settling in their chosen perches they have chosen for the night, this one majestic tree is now filled to overflowing with a mix of bird life. This is the moment they have gathered for; as the sky gives off one last flame of deep orange, the conductor lifts his wings; his long beak points up to the sky. Unfolding his large majestic wings, they open as if in a wounded surrender that welcomes the dusk, it encourages birds on the gum tree in all the many mixes and breeds of birdlife to give one finale salute to the day, it swells in a huge crescendo, each small chest puffed out with effort, each beak wide open, the sound thrills those that are too young to join in, then slowly silence, not one sound or peep, not one rustle or peck in that one space in time, not one sound for a micro second, then it's gone, lost forever as the day changes to night. As always one grumpy Kula fusses around, finding another more comfortable place on the branch.

Soon every bird on every branch had settled into slumber, that is until the Conductor unexpectedly chose to go solo, his loud baritone voice began to sing out with the single beat of Ro-Ro-Ro, it was neither musical nor was it entertaining it was simply annoying. The flock that adored now surrounded him, they began to complain, some breaking of twigs to prod him, calling out "It's nighttime, be quiet, go to sleep" but the Heron would not, on and on he sang, until anger built amongst the Kulahs who had gathered, pushing him off the tree into the lake below.

The Heron lay in the shallows, dazed, not knowing why those who claimed they followed him would want to harm him, when he was the best conductor. The one who always gave sage advice? The one who they turned to for his profound wisdom? Why had they betrayed him and attacked him? He limped away bruised in body and heart. The next day, the Heron limped to the wise owl's abode, asking the question that had haunted him all night. The Wise Owl's advice was this: "Remember my words, Heron, anyone can adore you when the stars are shining on you; however, it's when the storm breaks, that is where you will learn who truly cares for you." Heron did not understand.

He had been told he was a born leader, a patriarch within his flock. He wandered in the shallows of the great lake Tagimaucia, wondering why his song voice had annoyed his followers. The day passed quickly. His attendance was expected at dusk as the conductor, yet Heron refused to return to where he was so disliked.

The wide-eyed Owl flew to an overhanging branch. "They are expecting you. Why do you not return to conduct? "The Heron had had all day to think about the wise Owl's words.

So, within the Heron's newly found wisdom, he replied, "They soon will find another to conduct the days farewell, for now I am content to be silent, to become part of what they witness and listen to what my heart whispers.

The End

Motto

For The Conductor

It matters not what others think of you when you know you have done the right thing. Building a belief in yourself is the foundation for greatness. No one should make you feel inferior without your consent. It's not who you are that holds you back; it's who you think you're not.

SeaPearl

The Little Mermaid

Fable 6

A Very Long Time Ago

The old woman did not want to leave her wind-worn cabin by the sea, as on this day she felt so very tired, but to do her daily jobs of collecting firewood to keep her warm, she knew she should make the effort. Her little cottage was built from the wood of many shipwrecks. It sat squat and solid on a small hillock overlooking the Pacific Ocean, its crooked chimney belched out smoke in large puffs, which the strong sea wind whipped up into the sky and far away. Small, crooked windows were made up of numerous coloured bottles once washed up by the sea, the door and lintel each telling a story of their far distant travels.

Elsie had been born in this house and always loved it; she had never wanted to live anywhere else but here, by the tumbling waves of the Pacific Ocean. She was known far and wide as she was the last of the Northland *Seaweed Pickers*. Being much older than anyone else she knew, Elsie mainly wandered the shore happy to listen to the waves and discuss the day with her friends the seagulls. She was more than content as everything she ever wanted was right here by the sea.

Elsie had always loved to collect rare Shells and often found so much seaweed that she would dry it in the hot sun then sell it at the local markets. The farmers loved to buy seaweed it was very good for their plants. "Life is full of surprises," Elsie would often say to herself when she found a special shell. But one winters day the treasure Elsie found was not a rare shell, it was a rare treasure.

You see, one night there was a huge storm, one of the biggest storms Elsie had ever witnessed. The wind had screamed and moaned about her little house; it had raged all night sending the waves crashing against the shore with a thunderous boom. The next morning, once the storm had passed, Elsie decided to collect firewood. She did not want to get cold, so she put on a large tartan coat, with huge black shiny buttons down its front, a bright green woolly scarf which she wrapped around her head, grey mittens on her hands, and big red gumboots to stomp through the sand.

She found a small sack to put her firewood in and off she trudged, her gumboots crunching on the sand, small crabs darting out of the way, of her big rubber boots. She did not have to go far from home to find what she needed; she could already see big lumps of driftwood. She always felt this small tickle of excitement in her chest; the sea would deliver a beautiful shell. The seagulls were already squawking at one another, arguing over the fishy bits and pieces to be found. Large crabs were waving their claws at each other, warning the others that they would receive a nasty nip if they tried to steal their breakfast.

Overhead, Elsie saw that black storm clouds were gathering once more; little flickers of lightning flashed across the sky, casting strange shadows on the sand.

She spied a lot of broken wood, old barrels, and a small broken dinghy. Picking up all she could carry; Elsie shoved and squeezed the pieces into her sack until it bulged, her pockets were already full of smaller shells, her mind already busy creating another windchime with them.

As she began to return to the warmth of her cottage, she saw a large pale conch shell lying on the sand, this was indeed a beautiful rare treasure, she longed to take it home. She wondered what to do, if she added it in her sack of wood, it might chip or break it, however as she pondered, she heard a sound, like a baby bird calling out. Curious, Elsie shuffled around the pile of seaweed, looking for what had made that sound, the wind blowing so hard the old woman struggled to keep her balance; soon heavy drops of icy rain started to fall.

Another storm was on its way; it was time to hurry home. Elsie was about to walk away when she saw the tiniest pale pink hand caught in a matting of seaweed, 'I must be dreaming' Elsie thought. Gently pulling the large pile of seaweed apart to free it, the cries got stronger. Suddenly, Elsie gasped as there in front of her lay a baby mermaid tangled amongst the net and seaweed. Elsie quickly unwrapped her head scarf and put the tiny one inside. "What am I going to do with you? She thought as she gazed in wonder at this strange creature she held in her arms. The Babe was the colour of the ocean. Tiny silver scales grew from its tummy downwards ending in a small silver fish tail. Eyes of emerald green sparkled out from under dark eyelashes, brunette hair grew in curling whips over the child's head. From the moment Elsie had picked her up, the babies cries had stopped; trusting in this human to do the right thing.

Elsie began to make her way back to the cottage, the sack of wood forgotten. It was then that she realised, *this baby mermaid needs to be returned to the sea, not taken home.* Lighting and thunder still roamed around the sky growling like an angry tiger. All Elsie wanted to do was to hurry home and be by a warm fireplace with a hot cup of tea. But there was no other choice, Elsie was no swimmer; in fact, she did not like to get in the sea at all. *'I'm going to have to get wet,'* she thought reluctantly, *'There is no other way to put this little one back.'* Leaving her gumboots on the shore Elsie waded in up to her thighs, the icy sea water numbing her body. Terrible shivers raced up her spine, her tartan coat soaking up the water and weighing her down, chilling her to the bone.

She gasped as cold waves into splashed her face. One rouge wave washed over her, her body felt like it was frozen solid by the time she placed the tiny mermaid into the sea, watching as the little one wriggled in delight to be back in the watery world where she belonged. Before Elsie could blink another mermaid swam up and reached out for her child, then dived back into the waves, the mermaid baby had returned to the sea, where she belonged.

That night as Elsie sat dry and cozy in her warm cottage with hot cup of chocolate and two of her favourite chocolate biscuits. She thought about her day. *What an adventure that was, who would ever believe me?* She chuckled to herself, her toes now toasty-warm by a crackling fire, "I will call her my little *Sea Pearl,* hopefully we will meet again one day? Little did Elsie know that deep in the ocean, the child's father was gathering his great riches to show they were grateful for Elsie's kindness.

When she woke the next day, the sun was shining with the promised of a warm summer, Elsie opened her windows, to see on the sand bank where Elsies cottage was built, laying in the sand, a nest of the most beautiful shells, of all sizes, Elsie recognised a sea kings fortune had been gifted to her in return for the life of his beautiful SeaPearl.

Motto

SeaPearl

The Little Mermaid

If you give more than you receive, the abundance of kindness will always be within your reach.

If your abundance is shared, then your reward will be love.

If your love is shared, then you become immortal.

A Letter From The Author.

Dear reader, thank you for reading the South Pacific fables book. Collecting these stories and placing them where they will be read was a pleasure. My goal of this book was to help you remember the old stories you were told as children. Storytelling is a huge part of my life as a writer, and I find Fables and or fairy tales have a beginning seated deeply in the many countries that I have had the pleasure of visiting. So, I listen to their words, then weave them into a tapestry of stories that hopefully will not be lost in the future of this digital world. It is up to us to make sure this does not happen, by either visiting our libraries or purchasing from the publisher or author. I can promise you that this adult fable book will be entertaining as well as enlightening. It's been my absolute pleasure to write this book, knowing that many of you will relate to the Mottos I have included below each one. My next book, Dream Weavers, will be published in 2026; it is the second book of the Storytellers Series. In each country I've been a guest in, I've enjoyed a flirtation with their culture of weaving, all adding a flavour of richness to this story and the world we live in.

Dream Weavers

Book Two of the Story Tellers series

Tara loves her nomadic lifestyle, she has always acknowledged the power of storytelling, to her delight, weaving together customs and folktales comes naturally. To her, storytelling is living a fulfilling life. However, on her return to her homeland in Western Australia, she discovers that in her absence, her art community is now webbed with lies and deceit. Her once-friendly colleagues shunned her as wildfire gossip ran before her. Suddenly, her own family demands that she leave their home; Tara joins the ranks of the homeless. Is her nomadic lifestyle bought to a halt? Read on, as her love of storytelling and adventure go hand in hand. Always threading her pen with the ink of her imagination, until one day she discovers there is no bigger adventure than the one she has decided to explore, and once there, there may be no return.

Kez Wickham St George
The Dream Weavers
BOOK TWO OF THE
STORYTELLER SERIES

About The Author

'We are all Unique Walking Stories Just Waiting to be Told.'

Kez Wickham St George is a 5-Star Gold Award-Winning Best-Selling Author whose influence in the literary world is profound and far-reaching. Acclaimed as a highly gifted speaker, global writer's consultant, and leader in her profession, Kez's wisdom and passion have touched countless lives. Her dedication to championing people from diverse backgrounds to tell their stories and write with passion is at the core of her work.

With multiple best-selling books and two prestigious Gold Titan Awards to her name, Kez is recognised as a literary force to be reckoned with. Her storytelling prowess and commitment to creative writing have earned her numerous literacy awards and accolades, including the People's Choice Able Book Awards. A true global citizen, Kez has spoken nationally and internationally, sharing her knowledge about the process of writing, editing, and producing all forms of written communication. She is widely travelled, and her experiences have shaped her expansive authorship, encouraging others to think outside the box and redefine what authors can achieve in the digital age.

Kez's work has been celebrated by two royal families in the UK and Sweden, and she either coordinated and coauthored over twelve anthologies, including one on the lives of eighteen international women and another with Michiko Sato, featuring authors and artists from Ako, Japan. With fourteen books to her name, including a celebrated trilogy, a collection of poems and quotes, and a recent anthology with #mmhpress, this book is her first book of Fables.

Kez continues to captivate readers with her diverse and compelling narratives. In her Western Australian community, Kez is known for her efforts to empower others to write, creating writers' workshops and giving back through her volunteer work with Global Book Reviews. She has co-produced and co-hosted a weekly international show that highlights the work of authors and artists from around the world. Her creative energies and refreshing idealism are reflected in her consistent dedication to her craft, culminating in a short film adaptation of the prologue from her novel Scribe, which was shown in theatres across Australia.

Beyond her literary achievements, Kez is a prominent figure in the media, contributing to numerous magazines and co-hosting TV and radio shows where she shares her passion for personal development and women's global access to resources. Kez believes in the power of education for all women globally, seeing it as the key to achieving equality. She encourages everyone to express themselves through art, no matter the genre, and her favourite quote, *we are all unique walking stories just waiting to be told'* embodies her approach to life and work.

Ready to elevate your writing career?

Contact Kez for expert mentoring, book promotion, or to gain visibility through her renowned book reviews. With her extensive experience and passion for storytelling, Kez is here to help you gain the recognition you deserve.

www.kezwickhamstgeorge.com

Book Awards and Reviews

The Story Tellers Series

Jigsaw

Book 1 in the Storytellers Series 2023

Literary Titan Review ☆☆☆☆☆☆

Kez Wickham St George is an engrossing and emotionally charged narrative that delves into the Deeply concealed world of Parental childhood Trauma. At the heart of this tale is Cassie, the protagonist who endures a life riddled with abuse and neglect within the confines of her family home, desperately yearning. For love and acceptance. Compelled into a marriage with a narcissistic alcoholic as a result of her families Cult like obligations. Cassie is faced with the bleak choice of either succumbing to despair or embarking. On a courage journey to discover her true self. Throughout the narrative the author skilfully Weaves themes of escape, love, resilience, and the Patriarchal systems cruel oppression while exploring the enigmatic paranormal aspects that entwine themselves in Cassie's life. Jigsaw is a poignant, gripping Masterpiece, adeptly unwavering the profound story of a child growing through the profound abuse into the success story we have before us today.

Tapestry

Book 2 in the Storytellers Series 2024

Literary Titan Review

Tapestry is an intricate, multi-generational tale that weaves together the stories of women who have been marginalised and oppressed but are fiercely resilient. Set against the backdrop of historical periods where patriarchy, sexism, and injustice reigned supreme, the book tells the stories of women like Aida and Rosalie, whose lives were marked by pain but also by fortitude and wisdom. At its core, the book is a tribute to the strength of ancestral female wisdom and the persistence of the human spirit. What struck me immediately was the rawness of the storytelling. There's something visceral in how the author portrays Aida's life in the 1700s. The imagery of her as a child left to survive in a pigpen, later abused, and sold, but ultimately rising to become a healer, was both heartbreaking and triumphant. The writing captures not just the brutality of her circumstances, but also her inner strength and resilience, particularly when she delivers babies and saves lives with her herbal knowledge.

While the stories are compelling, the pacing in some sections, like Petra's story in the convent, was slower and more introspective, while other parts, such as the vivid descriptions of Rosalie's journey on the convict ship, were packed with action and emotion. The lengthy descriptions and heavy use of historical context sometimes pulled me out of the emotional depth of the characters' journeys. I would've loved more balance between the historical backdrop and the intimate personal moments that define these women's lives.

Another standout element is how the book dives into themes of female solidarity. The interactions between Aida, Ursula, and the group of women they eventually join in the woods felt empowering. Despite being rejected by society, these women form their own community, sharing knowledge and supporting one another. That part of the book, to me, was a beautiful ode to the strength of women when they come together. The detailed descriptions of the forest life, food gathered, and herbal remedies they concocted made these scenes feel rich and alive.

Tapestry is a bold and sweeping story that showcases the harsh realities faced by women throughout history but also their incredible resilience and ability to thrive despite it all. I would recommend this book to readers who enjoy historical fiction with deep emotional depth and a strong focus on female empowerment.

Review by Annie Gibbins Women's Biz Global

"A Masterpiece of Resilience and Ancestral Legacy"

Kez Wickham St George has crafted a remarkable and evocative novel in Tapestry: The Book of Lost Worlds. This book is a profound exploration of the courageous women who defied societal norms, battled against the injustices of their times, and left an indelible mark on history. Wickham St George's storytelling prowess shines as she weaves together the lives of these women, creating a rich tapestry of narratives that are both heart-wrenching and inspiring.

Through the lens of these brave female ancestors, the novel delves into themes of resilience, strength, and the enduring impact of ancestral legacies. The author masterfully captures the emotional depth and complexities of each character, allowing readers to connect with their struggles and triumphs on a deep personal level. The vivid descriptions and historical contexts enrich the narrative, bringing to life the harsh realities faced by women who fought against the constraints of religion, sexism, and societal expectations.

The prose is lyrical and haunting, with each chapter serving as a testament to the fortitude of these women. Wickham St George's ability to intertwine these stories with a sense of reverence for the past makes Tapestry a compelling and unforgettable read. This book not only honours the memory of those who came before but also serves as a powerful reminder of the strength and resilience that lies within all of us.

Tapestry: The Book of Lost Worlds is more than just a historical novel; it is a celebration of the human spirit and the enduring power of storytelling. It is a must-read for anyone who appreciates rich, character-driven narratives that explore the complexities of history and the legacy of those who dared to stand against the tide. Kez Wickham St George has created a literary gem that will resonate with readers long after the final page is turned.

Review by Geoff Bailey USA book reviews

Tapestry book 2 of the Storyteller Trilogy by Kez St. George is a beautifully told series of stories from her family ancestral record. Each chapter and character captured beautifully with a caring authority that has shown compassion for the hard life of her ancestors. Being a huge genealogy fan and consider collections like Tapestry to be so important for us to understand who we are and where we come from. Reading Tapestry made me appreciate New Zealand where the Author originated from and now resides in Australia. I consider stories and memoirs like those in Tapestry such an important capture of a people, their cultures their lives, and their histories. I would go as far to say I found Tapestry a true national treasure, and no doubt a bestseller. Thank you for an entertaining and enlightening read Kez Wickham St. George.

The People's Choice Award

Able Book Awards

2024

The Campfire Trilogy

Metal Mermaid - *Book 1 of the series*

No #1 Amazon Best Seller in 5 categories and 6 countries

Titan Gold & Silver awards medallions
mmhpress Gold award
WA Literati recommendations award.

Literary Titan Review ⭑⭑⭑⭑⭑

Metal Mermaid 5-star Review by Titan by Kez Wickham St George is a beautifully written memoir that takes readers on a spiritual and physical adventure. Tara and her husband Russ set off on a journey to explore Western Australia, but unexpected events quickly change their plans. Tara's journey of self-discovery takes her on a new path, one that challenges her both physically and emotionally. She meets fellow travellers and experiences the joys of the caravanning world, making her way from Australia's upper coast to New Zealand's northern island.

In this thought-provoking book, Wickham St George skilfully weaves a tale of courage, resilience, and determination that is both inspiring and captivating. The author's descriptive writing style transports readers to the various locations Tara visits, allowing them to feel the change of seasons and experience the heat and cold of the land. The side characters in the book are equally intriguing, with rich backstories and tales of their own. Metal Mermaid is an immersive memoir that provides readers with clear insight into the caravanning world and introduces them to various cultures.

Wickham St George's straightforward writing style makes the book an easy and engaging read. The book is infused with culture and worldly sights, and readers will feel like they are part of Tara's journey. Metal Mermaid is an outstanding book that I highly recommend to readers looking for inspirational that showcases the beauty of life's Journey. The authors ability to tell such a captivating story that takes its readers on a spiritual journey is nothing short of Impressive. Metal Mermaid is an outstanding book that I highly recommend to readers looking for an inspirational book that highlights the beauty of life's journey. The author's ability to tell a captivating story that takes readers on a spiritual adventure is nothing short of an impressive literature experience.

The Cuppa Tree - Book 2 of the series

A story of a woman who lived loved and learned caravaning in the outback. Sit around the metaphorical campfire with author Kez Wickham St George as she brings you on an unexpected journey throughout the pages of The Cuppa Tree. This natural-born storyteller will share tales from experiences and stories shared on her travels around Australia.

Scribe

Book 3 of the series

When Tara, the lead character, finds herself battling illness and snowstorms in the far South Island of New Zealand, she is called a catalyst for what she is being asked to do: die. "The world is in a state of great change," she is told. We, the greater good, ask you to Scribe for the deceased, those who have not told their stories before they passed over.

Co- authored Anthology's

Hear us Roar 2025 KMD publisher. A bestselling anthology that brings the hearts together, powerful short stories told by an array of global authors.

55 faces Inspire 2024

No #1 Amazon Best Seller. An anthology that embraces many women of many dialects and ethnicities. An inspirational book that will have you reaching out to be part of the next book due out in 2025

Rising into greatness by worthy women.com 2025.

No #1 Amazon Best Seller. A collection of heartwarming stories who will inspire you to live life on your terms.

Memoirs of Successful Women

Memoirs of Successful Women is a collection of stories from women who have lived, breathed, and elevated their brand.

Women's Biz Publishing. 2023

The Colors of Me

The Colors of Me is a multinational contribution of 18 authors, each one sharing her empowering and inspirational story.

Inspired Connections

Unleashing the Magic of Deeper Relationships

No #1 Amazon in 37 categories – 2021/ 2023

There will be many roadblocks and many dysfunctions along the way. Your job in life is to sort out the noise and nonsense, to trust your intuition and acknowledge your own truth.

Hille House Publishing. 2021

Build Your Success

Leadership Tips from the World's Best CEO's and Leaders

A co-authored book that sheds light on leadership and many success tips from the world's best leaders and Mentors. Critical thinkers and role models who have proven success, built on ideology plus uncovering the essential tools for risk-taking, goal setting, and most of all purpose.

Testimonials of Mentorship

From Sandy Skelton Publisher / Editor Ozark.

There is simply something magical about Kez. She is brilliant, honest, transparent, and forthright. From the moment we met, I knew I'd found a kindred spirit whose mission is to extend a hand to lift up others following in our footsteps or carving their own similar path. Kez reviewed my publishing house Ozark Press's first publication The Power to Rise Above. That experience ensured that she will be a part of my writer's journey forevermore. At whatever stage you are at in your writing journey, engaging Kez in your project will improve it immeasurably. You are in safe hands. With more sharks out there in the book coaching arena, it is refreshing to meet a genuine soul like Kez who wants your book to shine and openly shares her extensive knowledge and expertise

From Nicola Mary Burton. Author of 'The One.

To Kez Wickham St George Publisher. There's not enough space, to say what my heart feels for your dedication, your hours of work, creativity, teachings, guidance, wisdoms, inspirations, The beginning of first the few words that I gave you, that you magically transformed for this book. A profound mentor, coach, and structural editor. More importantly, your ability to see me, in my true colours and vulnerability. For being my safe harbor throughout the many storms, I traversed in the true spirit of writing. I thank you, with all my beingness, for who I have become, as a writer and published author. I will continue to aspire, to dig deep into my inner muse, as you are forever my Guiding Inspiration.

From Patti Stueland Author of 'Living Your Best Dash.'

A part of living your best Dash, are the people you choose to surround yourself with. God has blessed me with so many incredible people over my lifetime and continues to do so. One of those incredible blessings has been to meet and collaborate with my structural editor and co-publisher Kez Wickham St. George. I first met Kez as a guest on my podcast, "Rediscovering your Passion and Purpose with Patti." Listening to her talk about how enthusiastic she is about helping women to tell their stories really touched me deeply. When I knew it was time to get going on this project, Kez was the first person I thought of to share this DASH book idea. She loved it.

Through her guidance, encouragement, support, and knowledge, I have now recently completed my book Living Your Best Dash, where my mentor Kez Wickham St George has been the catalyst for me in achieving this amazing goal. Even though Kez lives in Australia, and I live in the United States, together we have made this book become a reality, one of the fantastic things about technology! If you are looking to achieve your goal of authoring a book and especially want to share your story, then Kez Wickham St. George is the one you want as your structural editor / Publisher. She is an absolute joy to work with; I highly recommend Kez!